Oh Dear!

Rod Campbell

MACMILLAN CHILDREN'S BOOKS

Buster went to stay
with Grandma on the farm.
Grandma asked Buster
to fetch the eggs.

So he went to the barn
and asked the . . .

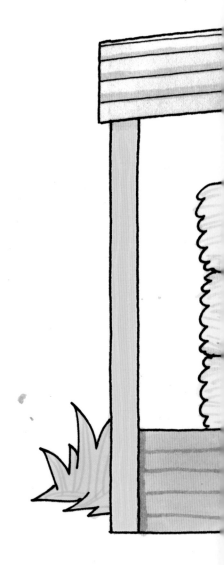

No eggs here!
Oh dear!

So he went to the sty
and asked the . . .

No eggs here!
Oh dear!

So he went to the field
and asked the . . .

No eggs here!
Oh dear!

So he went to the stable
and asked the . . .

No eggs here!
Oh dear!

So he went to the kennel
and asked the . . .

No eggs here!
Oh dear!

So he went to the hutch
and asked the . . .

No eggs here!
Oh dear!

So he went to the pond
and asked the . . .

No eggs here!
Oh dear!

Then Buster remembered!
So he went to the henhouse
and asked the . . .

Lift me up!
Hooray!